Arth

Arthur and the Twrch Trwyth

Margaret Isaac

Margaret Isaac

Illustrations:
Margaret Jones

APECS PRESS CAERLEON

First published in 2012 by APECS Press

Published in Wales by
APECS Press, Caerleon, Newport, NP18 3QZ
e-mail: apecsmarak@aol.com
www.apecspress.co.uk
Tel: 01633 852944
Fax: 01633 858161

ISBN 978-0-9563965-4-9 (Hardback)
ISBN 978-0-9563965-3-2 (Paperback)

Printed in Wales by
Dinefwr Press, Llandybïe, Carmarthenshire

For Alun

and

the communities who keep the stories alive

Contents

The Quest

Hunting the Twrch Trwyth

Acknowledgements

THE WRITING OF this book started as part of a planned series of books describing the folktales associated with some of the lakes of Wales. I was attracted to the story of a youthful, adventurous, heroic Arthur engaged in hunting a ferocious wild boar across south Wales, the land of my birth! Moreover, Arthur's hunt fell within the vicinity of three lakes which had come within my earlier research and was also one of the first known records of Arthur. I had already written about two of the lakes, Llyn Llech Owain, near Gorslas, and Llyn-y-Fan Fawr in the Black Mountain of the Brecon Beacons; I discovered the existence of Llyn Lliwan in the Severn Estuary near Chepstow for the first time! Dr Robin Gwyndaf, Honorary Research Fellow at the National Museum of Welsh Life, St Fagans, has offered staunch support and encouragement of the lakes project, and I am indebted to him for giving his valuable time to proofreading and editing some of my earlier work.

The story of Culhwch and Olwen is the backdrop to the Hunting of the Twrch Trwyth; I had read some earlier translations of the *Mabinogion*, which includes this story and was invited to a talk by Professor Sioned Davies, Head of the School of Welsh at Cardiff University about her new translation. Her talk was inspiring and a subsequent meeting was the beginning of a much valued friendship. In subsequent discussions, her advice, guidance and unfailing encouragement has ensured that this book will help the contemporary audience to an understanding of the robustness and excitement of life in the time of Arthur and his knights. Her translation has been invaluable, and it is with deep gratitude that I express my thanks to Professor Davies for her unstinting support, including reading the text prior to publication and for her remarks in the Foreword.

I wish to mention my special friendship with Margaret Jones of Aberystwyth, artist and book illustrator. As in previous publications, Margaret has given permission to use her beautiful and dynamic illustrations in the book and provided additional advice on matters of text and dress of the period. Many of the illustrations used have been published previously in the books, *Culhwch ac Olwen* and *The Quest for Olwen* and were first published by the University of Wales Press. A small part of the Mabinogion poster map is printed by kind permission of the National Library Wales, Aberystwyth. Some illustrations used are from the privately-owned paintings of Belinda Humfrey, Desborough, Northamptonshire and Peter Jones, Aberystwyth, Ceredigion.

Dr Bronwen Price, Project Development Officer, Literature Wales, has always been approachable and offered sound advice and support, and I am particularly grateful to her for promoting my materials on the Literature Wales website. I also express my gratitude to the librarians of the National Library of Wales, Cardiff Main Library and Malpas Library, Newport.

I have been able to call on the expertise and experience of many others: Dr Tony Ramsay, Director of the Fforest Fawr Geopark, Alan Bowring, Geopark Project Development Officer and colleagues of the Brecon Beacons National Park, Sian Tucker, Administrative Officer, the Black Mountain Centre, Brynaman, and David Davies (Daidoc), Clerk of Cwmamman Council. I am fortunate to have received their help and goodwill for which I am grateful.

In my travels and research into folktales around Wales, I have talked with many people in the local communities. They have gladly shared their memories and anecdotes of the folktales of their own localities and I thank them for their help and inspiration. The interpretive display panels of Arthur's chase of the Twrch Trwyth currently being erected in the Amman Valley are based to some extent on this relationship with the local people.

Lastly, I thank my family and friends who have given me constant support over many years, especially my husband, Alun, for his support, patience and understanding.

Foreword

How Culhwch won Olwen is one of eleven medieval Welsh tales known as the *Mabinogion* and is one of the finest examples of the Welsh storytelling tradition. Centred on the two classical international themes of the 'Jealous Stepmother' and the 'Giant's Daughter', it relates how Culhwch, with the help of Arthur, overcomes his stepmother's curse to marry Olwen, daughter of Ysbaddaden Chief Giant. But in order to win the maiden, the young hero must accomplish many seemingly impossible tasks of which hunting the magical boar Twrch Trwyth is one. As the boar and his piglets are chased from Ireland, across south Wales, and eventually to Cornwall, they leave a trail on the landscape so that place-names are a constant reminder of the legend.

This boar hunt is the focus of Margaret Isaac's retelling of the tale, directed at both children and adults. Her fluent style successfully conveys the energy and humour of the original text, while Margaret Jones' illustrations visually entice the reader into a world populated by giants, hags, and warriors such as Canhastyr Hundred-Hands, Sgilti Lightfoot and Gwiawn Cat-Eye. Moreover, this new version serves as a reminder of our rich heritage and culture, and of how our traditional stories are very firmly rooted in the Welsh landscape. Without doubt, readers will be inspired to visit locations on the wild boar's trail so that they can see for themselves where Grugyn was killed or where the Twrch Trwyth was ambushed by Arthur and his warriors, so investing this fascinating medieval tale with a lasting significance.

Professor Sioned Davies
Chair of Welsh
Cardiff University

Introduction

CULHWCH AND OLWEN is a vibrant story which is in essence a series of tales held together by the gossamer thread of the timeless folktale of a lover seeking the giant's daughter, a story that is short on detail but ever present throughout.

I was attracted by this earliest known writing of the legendary Arthur, who with an army of warriors, experienced many magical adventures and finally sought to overcome the otherworld creature, the Twrch Trwyth, a story that is firmly rooted in the landscape of south Wales. Strange magical gods and heroes, giants, and fabulous animals come to life in a tale of cunning, sorcery and witchcraft, pitted against the courage of Arthur and his warriors.

Many of the characters possess mythical attributes: Cai's ability to survive underwater; Clust, Gwiawn Cat-Eye and Sgilti Lightfoot with gifts of hearing, sight and speed respectively, Menw the spell maker, and the extremely useful Gwrhyr who had the gift of tongues. These characters make an appearance in many other stories captured in early Welsh manuscripts, and thanks to scholarly translations, they have been made accessible to those Welsh people, who are now unable to speak their original mother tongue, and to all who enjoy such enchanting tales.

I have long had an interest in stories connected with places and Wales is full of such stories. I very much enjoy visiting the places I intend to write about, and I discover many new and exciting things, such as the places and tales which led to my writing the story *Arthur and the Twrch Trwyth.* I was particularly drawn to a tale that is so embedded in the landscape of south Wales where many places record the characters and incidents in the story. For example, Kynwas the Lame is attacked by the Twrch Trwyth early in the story and is possibly remembered in the place name Canaston near Narberth; Arthur's chase of the Twrch Trwyth into the Preseli Mountains is commemorated by place names like Carn Arthur, Moel Dyrch, Tre Dyrch; St. Clears, the Welsh name, Sanclêr, is possibly derived from the French word *le sanglier* meaning wild boar, the fact that this is the point in the story when Arthur calls on the help of the French King, Gwilenhin, lends some credence to this claim.

When the hunt reaches the Amman Valley the battle reaches a climax that probably accounts for the many names in this area meaning boar or sow – Amman and Amanw derive from *y banw* the Welsh word for boar and there are also places called Twyn y Moch, Llwyn y Moch, Cwmtwrch; Ffrydiau Twrch; Banwen Place, Garth Grugyn and River Egel – the name deriving from Echel Fforddwyd Twll (Echel Mighty Thigh in English) who was one of the warriors who died in battle. This is a remarkable example of the way in which such stories of Wales are rooted in place names.

In *Arthur and the Twrch Trwyth,* I have accentuated the story of the hunt against the backdrop of the story of Culhwch and Olwen. I have created some descriptions of the battle incidents which do not exist in the original story. For example, the battles at Nevern are imagined as having taken place in wet and gloomy conditions to convey the desolation felt by a father for his son as Arthur mourns the death of his son Gwydre. Similarly, when the hunters and the boars are engaged in battle, the methods of boar hunting are described in more detail than is given in the original tale.

The book is written for every adult and child who responds to the gusto of Arthur and his warriors, to the vibrant sweep of the action, to the fantastic and the grotesque, and the poignancy of the vulnerability and exquisite beauty of Olwen, held in the castle of Ysbaddaden, her father, until she is released and brought to life by her lover.

It is written for the reader who engages with the cruelty and viciousness of Ysbaddaden yet can recognise the squeak of pathos when his death comes, in fact, it is written for the reader from any walk of life who simply enjoys an uplifting, audaciously exuberant and magical story.

Margaret Isaac

In the beginning, when any form of travel was a great adventure in itself, one of the earliest means of communication shared between countries was the folk-tale. Storytellers would carry tales told by their own firesides to foreign hearths, picking up additional stories along the way and adding them to their own. Such a story is that of Culhwch and Olwen, the earliest recorded tale of Arthur and his warriors. In the ensuing centuries the characters of Arthur and his men were to become great favourites throughout Europe in the expanding cult of romantic chivalry, and have continued to inspire artists and writers to the present day.

Margaret Isaac has retold the story of the Hunting of the Twrch Trwyth against the background of the story of Culhwch and Olwen and added fresh insight and imagination to the hunting incidents. She used the illustrations first created for the *Mabinogion* and the Quest for Olwen in a fresh and original manner to point up her unique approach to the story, for example, the cover design uses a part of the illustration from the *Mabinogion* to accentuate the story of the hunt, and the crescendo of fighting which took place in the Amman Valley and the Severn Estuary are enhanced by her careful selection of illustrations.

I am delighted to be associated with her work, which offers a fresh insight into one of the most exciting Arthurian stories. It could well be argued that Wales' best-loved and longest lasting legend of King Arthur and his warriors, one of the earliest stories told, has lost none of its original charm over the years.

Margaret Jones

The Quest

Daylight and Shadows

It is said that the creature known in Wales long ago as the Twrch Trwyth was a gigantic magical boar with poisonous bristles and a vicious temper that ravaged Wales, carving his presence on the lakes, rivers, mountains and valleys, marks that can be seen to this very day. It seems that he was not, in fact, a boar at all, but a king who was changed into a boar as a penance for a great crime. Some say that the Twrch Trwyth led the dead to the edge of the underworld, and pointed them to their last and final destination. Lodged between the ears of this great creature was a comb, a razor and a pair of scissors.

The fascinating tale of the hunting of the Twrch Trwyth begins when Culhwch, cousin to Arthur, the High King, fell in love with Olwen, a maiden so beautiful that it was said that whoever saw her would be filled with love for her.

Culhwch's father was King Cilydd and his mother was the daughter of the leader known as Lord Amlawdd. Her name was Goleuddydd (or Daylight as she is known in English), a name which reflected her sunny and loving nature. She bore Cilydd a child, a son named Culhwch. After he was born, she became very ill, and before she died, she became anxious for her son's wellbeing, should her husband marry again. She feared that a second wife would try to come between Culhwch and his father, Cilydd, and so rob him of his inheritance.

Daylight was afflicted with bouts of madness, and did not like being confined within any building. She was often found wandering the countryside. On one such occasion, her husband was leading her gently back to her home, when she clutched his hand and looked up into his face weeping piteously.

"Please don't cry so," said Cilydd, "I cannot bear to see you so unhappy."

"Oh my husband," she sobbed, "I am afraid that I have not long to live and I am anxious about our son's future."

"I hope you will recover and live long, my dearest wife," said he, "but even if that were not possible, why would you think that Culhwch would be in danger, when I am here to protect him?"

"I am afraid that if you marry again, a second wife will not care for Culhwch as we have done," she said. "I would like to ensure that you do not rush into such a marriage, so I want you to promise me that after my death, you will not take a wife until you see two bramble bushes growing on my grave."

"Such silly fancies," cried her husband, but he could see that she was greatly upset and went on reassuringly, "of course I will promise if it sets your mind at rest and I will keep my word."

Daylight was satisfied that Cilydd was a man of his word, but, she wanted to make doubly sure, so the next day, she sought out a private meeting with her priest and asked him to promise her that when she died he would see that her grave was regularly tended so that nothing would grow on it.

"Of course I will," said the priest, "you do not need to ask."

"I know I can trust you," said Daylight, "and I would feel at peace knowing that you were keeping my memory alive for Cilydd and for my son Culhwch."

She did not give him her true reason for this request.

Cilydd kept his promise and everyone in his household knew of his vow and respected his wishes. The grave remained bare for seven years, but then the priest became careless, and one day, Cilydd's servant, Gwyn, who passed by the grave on his way to his master's house, noticed that two bramble bushes were growing on the grave. It surprised him because the grave had hitherto been well kept. He hastened to inform his master, thinking that perhaps he would want them removed:

"My lord," he said, "the grave of your beloved wife Goleuddydd, has always been beautifully kept, free from weeds and brambles, as I am sure you would wish. I noticed today that two bramble bushes are growing on it, would you wish me to remove them?"

Surprised and interested Cilydd replied, "No Gwyn, I think that this might have been ordained, leave the grave as it is."

He remembered his wife's words, "I want you to promise me that after my death, you will not take a wife until you see two bramble bushes growing on my grave."

He believed that he was released from his promise to his dead wife and that he was now free to marry again.

Cilydd began to seek advice from members of his court and his steward, Menw, told him that he knew of a woman who might suit the king very well.

"She is the wife of King Doged," said he.

Now Cilydd had a long standing feud with this king so he ordered an expedition to kill King Doged and take possession of his land. They forcibly abducted his wife and brought her before Cilydd. She stood silently in front of him accompanied by her own young daughter. The king, pleased with her beauty, made her his wife.

After Daylight's death, Cilydd had placed his son Culhwch with foster parents, so his second wife did not know that he had a son. As Daylight had foreseen, the woman wished to promote her daughter's happiness and expected her to become Cilydd's heir. She was out walking one day, and began to ponder on her fate since she had been abducted from her own home. She felt lonely and homesick. She could not forget that her first husband, King Doged had been killed on Cilydd's orders.

She found that she had strayed far from Cilydd's house and was walking through some woods on his estate. She suddenly came upon a small house, outside an old woman sat quietly mending some clothes.

Cilydd's wife stopped to talk to the old woman.

"Good morning," she said, "do you mind if I stop here to rest?"

"Not at all, said the old woman, "I rarely see anybody, since I live here on my own, it is good to have someone to talk to."

"What is your name?" asked the old woman as Cilydd's wife sat beside her.

"My name is Arddu, I am married to Cilydd, lord of this estate.

"Ah!" said the old woman, "I know who you are! You are his second wife, his first wife, Daylight died tragically."

Arddu remained silent for a moment.

"Tell me," she said, "Did they have any children? Since I have been here, I have never seen any children or heard of any born from that marriage?"

Arddu assumed that the woman had lived in the neighbourhood all her life and would know something of Cilydd's past.

The old woman hesitated at first, she was naturally cautious and did not want to share confidences with Arddu who was a stranger to the area.

"I know of none," she said.

"Ah!" said the woman, "then, if they were childless, perhaps I too will be unable to bear any children for him and he will have no heir."

Arddu affected to look crestfallen. She was in fact a cunning and deceitful woman, and hoped induce the old woman to talk more freely.

"You may need have no worry about that," replied the old woman consolingly, "he may yet have an heir, and it may be by you." She was still a little cautious, and Arddu continued to look anxious and credulous. Unable to keep quiet any longer, the old woman burst out with the truth, "But, I believe he may have one son already."

"I am amazed," said Arddu, "I am glad I met you today, you have made me feel so much better and happier. I hope we meet again."

And so, Arddu left the old woman and returned home.

She sought out her husband immediately. "I have heard that you have a child already, why have you hidden him from me?" she asked. "Don't you trust me to look after him for you?"

Cilydd was perplexed and surprised. "I have no reason," he said, "I left him with foster parents when Daylight died. Perhaps he is now old enough to return home. It is time he was educated properly as befits a noble prince and heir to this royal estate."

Arddu believed that the best way of advancing her daughter's fortunes would be as the wife of Culhwch, and sought ways of bringing them together in the hope that Culhwch could be persuaded to marry her. Unfortunately, he did not find the daughter attractive, but he did not want to hurt her feelings, or offend his stepmother, so he tried to avoid the meetings the woman arranged to bring them together.

At last Arddu became impatient. "Do you not think it is time that you thought of taking a wife?" she said.

Culhwch blushed, he was very young and polite, "You are very kind to think of my happiness, stepmother," he said, "but I think that I may be too young to consider taking a wife. Perhaps I might think differently in a few years' time."

However, Arddu saw through his excuses and evasions and was furious with him for rejecting her daughter.

"I can see through your fine words," she said angrily, "I can see that you find my daughter repulsive, and you spurn my good intentions," she was in a great rage.

"I wanted the best for you," she ranted, "now I curse you. I swear that you will never marry unless you marry Olwen, the daughter of Ysbaddaden, Chief Giant."

As soon as she mentioned the name of Olwen, Culhwch was filled with an overwhelming desire to meet and marry this beautiful maiden, even though he had never seen her. Arddu's curse was taking effect.

Culhwch was a carefree and happy young man, but now he found he was unable to eat or sleep. He couldn't stop thinking about his love for Olwen and began to look quite thin and pale.

"What is the matter my son?" asked Cilydd.

Culhwch flushed with embarrassment.

"I have fallen hopelessly in love with Olwen, even though I have never seen her. I am sure that I will never be able to win her, and I cannot live without her."

"You will certainly do no good languishing here at court," said Cilydd, "you must seek her and win her. Ysbaddaden will not part with her easily, and he is a formidable enemy, so you must go to your cousin Arthur and ask him for his support."

At Arthur's Court

Culwch prepared to follow his father's advice and immediately set out for Arthur's court. He was seated on a gleaming grey horse with a gold bit in its mouth and a precious gold saddle on its back. Culhwch wore a purple cloak with a ruby gold ball in each corner, his buskin and stirrups were also made of precious gold. A gold-hilted sword rested on his thigh and he carried a gold-chased shield. Two spotted, white-breasted greyhounds ran in front of him, each one with a collar of red gold around its neck. He looked resplendent as he rode lightly into Arthur's court and called for the gatekeeper.

"Glewlwyd Mighty Grasp is my name and you may not enter Arthur's court until I have first announced you," said the gatekeeper.

So saying, he walked away.

"My lord Arthur," said Glewlwyd, "a warrior waits outside your gates. I do not know his name, but I have never seen such a handsome man before in my life."

"Then let him enter," said Arthur.

Culhwch rode boldly into the court and Arthur greeted him with kind and courteous words.

"You are welcome, sir," he said, "to come and share a meal with us, and to tell us who you are and where you come from."

"I am no beggar," replied Culhwch, "I am seeking your help, and if you grant what I ask of you, I promise that I shall be worthy of your favour."

"Gladly," the King replied.

"First, I want to have my hair trimmed," said Culhwch. This may seem a strange request, but his hair was very long as befitted his age, to have it trimmed would be a mark of his coming to manhood.

Arthur examined the young man curiously. He saw a handsome young man who bore himself with dignity and looked every inch a prince. He was wise and recognised that this was no ordinary man, and that his strange request was one of some significance. So, Arthur picked up a golden comb and scissors with loops of silver and began to comb and cut the young man's hair.

"I see by your looks and dress that you are no common man, may I know your name?" he said. "Your looks and demeanour tells me that you may be related to me by blood."

"My name is Culhwch, I am the son of Cilydd and Daylight."

"Then you are my cousin," said Arthur. "Name whatever you want and you shall have it."

Solemnly, Culhwch began to name Arthur's warriors, one by one, they numbered two hundred. Finally, he said:

"I want you to call on all these warriors and I want you to get me Olwen, daughter of Ysbaddaden, Chief Giant."

Arthur's Champions

ARTHUR SENT messengers to the far ends of every land to seek for Olwen. He expected her to be living with Ysbaddaden, her father, but his castle was not easy to find.

After seeking her for more than a year, without success, Culhwch became impatient.

"It seems to me that it would be better if I leave you and go on alone," he said angrily, "you have failed to honour your pledge to me, to seek and find Olwen; your great reputation has been gravely injured by your broken promises." Culhwch was so disappointed and frustrated that his words were very bitter.

"You insult Arthur far more than he deserves," said Cai, one of Arthur's bravest warriors. "Be patient, stay with us, and we will search for Olwen until we find her, or until you will have to admit that the maiden does not exist; we will stay by your side until then."

Cai Hir (Cai the Tall in English), was one of Arthur's chief warriors. His outstanding talents were well known. He was an excellent swimmer and could hold his breath underwater for days on end! He needed very little sleep, and could overcome extreme heat and extreme cold. He was also deadly with the sword, but he could sometimes be as quick-tempered as Culhwch.

Cai's words pacified Culhwch, and Arthur continued on the quest.

Many of Arthur's warriors were endowed with unique skills that would be indispensable in the tasks that lay ahead. Among these were Cynddylig the Guide (he was such a good tracker, he could find his way anywhere in the world), Gwrhyr, Interpreter of Languages (he was even able to speak the languages of birds and animals), and Gwalchmai, the Hawk (who never gave up until he had finished the task he had set himself); he was Arthur's nephew, his sister's son. Two of his greatest champions were Menw, the spell maker (he could make himself or other people invisible) and Bedwyr, Arthur's closest friend, handsome and invincible, and an outstanding spear thrower.

As these great heroes travelled over the bare countryside, Cai saw on the horizon a huge fort. As they came closer, they saw a flock of sheep, a shepherd and an enormous dog, larger than a full grown stallion.

Cai said to Gwrhyr, "Speak to that man in his language, and try to get him to help us."

"I don't like the look of the man or his dog," said Gwrhyr, nervously, "I think we should all go together."

"Have no fear," said Menw, "I will cast a spell on the dog and the man, and they will be unable to harm you," which he did.

So they approached the shepherd and Gwrhyr spoke to him.

"You look prosperous," said he, pointing to the large flock of sheep.

"Yes, I am," agreed the shepherd, "I prosper in my work, but my wife has been my undoing."

Gwrhyr, ignored the man's complaint about his wife.

"Whose sheep are you tending? And who is the lord of that great fort?" he asked.

"You must be strangers here," said the shepherd, "otherwise you would know that the fort belongs to Ysbaddaden, Chief Giant."

"Indeed," said Gwrhyr, "and what is your name?"

"I am Custennin, Ysbaddaden is my brother, and, because of my wife, he has ruined me. And what is your name and who are the warriors with you?"

"We are messengers of Arthur, seeking Olwen, the daughter of Ysbaddaden."

"Oh! No! May God protect you!" replied Custennin, he shuddered. "No-one in the world has come to make that request and left alive."

He rose and turned to leave, but Culhwch stopped him and offered him a ring as a token of his appreciation of the man's friendliness, which Custennin accepted.

On arriving home, Custennin showed his wife the ring and told her of his meeting with Culhwch and his companions. She was extremely surprised when she examined the ring.

"I would know this ring anywhere," she said excitedly, "it belonged to my sister Daylight," she cried. "She must be dead, for she would not have parted from her ring. She was married to Cilydd and her son is Culhwch."

"Culhwch is coming here with his comrades. He has fallen in love with Olwen and is seeking her and her father to ask his permission to wed her," said Custennin.

"I will be very pleased to see my nephew," she said, "but I am sorry to be meeting him in these circumstances, we both know that no-one who has made that attempt has ever left Ysbaddaden's fort alive."

The Beautiful Olwen

CULHWCH AND HIS friends received a warm welcome when they arrived at Custennin's home, where they enjoyed a good supper. When they had finished their meal, as the warriors were talking with Custennin, they noticed his wife walking quietly towards a dark corner of the room; she approached a large chest. She opened the chest and to the great surprise of Culhwch and the rest of the company, a young boy with golden hair climbed out.

"You are a handsome lad," said Gwrhyr, who was the first to recover his composure, "why are you hiding there?"

"He is the only son I have left," said the woman. "Twenty-three of my sons were killed by Ysbaddaden; I hide him here, to try to keep him safe, otherwise, this young lad may suffer the same fate as his brothers."

"If you will allow him to become my companion," said Cai, "he may like to accompany us, I promise that I will take good care of him. He will learn to become a trusted warrior of Arthur."

"Where will you be taking him?" asked the woman.

"We are seeking Ysbaddaden's fort and will ask him to allow Culwch to marry Olwen."

"For God's sake, turn back!" begged the woman, "I have lost twenty-three sons, and have good reason to know that you are facing the greatest danger! No-one has seen you yet from the fort, there is still time for you to escape."

"We won't turn back until we have seen the maiden," said Cai resolutely. "We may then judge for ourselves whether the quest is worth pursuing. Culhwch has never seen her and will not turn back until he has met her. Do you know of a way in which we may meet her, before we attempt to get inside Ysbaddaden's fort?"

The woman could see that they would not be easily persuaded to change their minds.

"She comes here every Saturday to wash her hair at the well," she replied reluctantly.

"Will she come if you send for her?"

"If you give me your word that you will do her no harm," said the woman, "I will see what I can do."

"We promise on our honour as Arthur's champions, that we will do her no harm," Cai said solemnly.

So the woman sent for Olwen, and Arthur's champions watched silently as she approached and they marvelled at her beauty. She wore a dress of flame red silk, with a necklace of red gold encrusted with precious pearls and red jewels about her neck. Her hair was golden yellow like the flowers of the broom, and her face, her arms and her neck were whiter than the white foam of the sea. Her eyes were more beautiful than the eyes of a young hawk. Her breasts were whiter than the breast of a young white swan and her cheeks redder than a foxglove. Four white clovers sprang up behind her wherever she went, and that was why she was given the name of Olwen, which means 'white track'.

She came into the house and sat by Culhwch. Culhwch gazed at her, his eyes filled with love.

"Maiden," he said, "I love you with all my heart, may I take you with me so that you will live with me always?"

"I cannot," she replied, "until I have asked my father. I have given him my word that I will ask his permission before I marry, for his very life depends on it. You must go to him and ask for my hand. Whatever he asks of you, you must promise to do it; if you succeed, I will be your bride, but if you fail in any way, you will not have me and you will be lucky to escape with your life."

Culhwch took her hand, "I will do everything you say," he said earnestly, "and I vow to you that I will succeed and I will claim you as my bride."

So Olwen left him, and returned home.

Ysbaddaden, Chief Giant

CULHWCH, ARTHUR, and his warriors, immediately made their way to the giant's fortress and forced their way through the gates and into the great hall.

Culhwch stood before Ysbaddaden with Arthur's champions behind him.

With one voice they shouted, "Greetings, Ysbaddaden, Chief Giant, Culhwch, cousin to Arthur, has come to seek your daughter as his bride."

"Who is that?" growled the giant, "where are my useless servants? Raise the forks under my eyelids so that I can see my prospective son-in-law." His servants rushed to obey him, pushing up each eyelid with a huge fork. Ysbaddaden glared at Culhwch and his friends.

"Come back tomorrow," he said, "I will give you an answer then."

As they turned to go, he snatched one of three poisoned spears beside him and hurled it after them but Bedwyr swiftly caught it and hurled it back. It pierced Ysbaddaden right through his kneecap. The giant howled with pain and hurled curses after them as they strode away.

Arthur's men spent the night in the house of Custennin and returned the following day.

"Ysbaddaden," they cried, "give Culhwch your daughter's hand in marriage. Unless you do this you shall meet your death."

"I must consult with her grandparents," grumbled the giant.

"Do that," they replied, "we will take a meal and return for your answer."

As they got up, he took the second stone spear and hurled it after them. This time Menw caught it and hurled it back. It pierced the giant in the middle of the chest so that it came right through to the middle of his back. The giant, in a frenzy of pain, hurled the most repulsive curses at them. And so they went away for a second time.

The third day they returned once more.

"Ysbaddaden, do not try to hurt us again, it will only bring you misery and grief." They tried to soothe the giant's bad temper. "Listen to what we have to say, before any further harm is done." Their sober words did not curb the giant's bad temper.

"Where are my servants," he growled, "to push the forks beneath my eyelids, my eyelids have fallen down over my eyes again and I cannot see the man who seeks to marry my daughter."

Culhwch stood before him once more, with his friends on either side, but the giant reached for the third stone spear and viciously flung it at them. Culhwch swiftly caught it and hurled it back and it pierced Ysbaddaden in the eyeball and came out through the nape of his neck, and he howled with pain.

Then the champions left the fort once more and returned to the house of Custennin.

They returned to the giant's court the following day.

"Ysbaddaden," they said, "we appeal to you, do not bring death on yourself. We ask only that you give your daughter, Olwen, to Arthur's cousin, Culhwch."

Sullenly, Ysbaddaden replied. "Where is the one who seeks her?"

"Here I am," said Culhwch.

"Come closer to me," said the giant, "Before I allow you to take my daughter, give me your word that you will get whatever I ask of you."

Ysbaddaden looked intently at the handsome youth standing before him. Culhwch stood before the giant, composed and dignified.

"So you are the one who seeks my daughter," growled the giant.

"I am Culhwch, son of Cilydd and Daylight, cousin of Arthur," replied Culhwch.

"You must give me your solemn oath that you will not deceive me."

"You have it."

"Then, so be it," said Ysbaddaden. "When you perform all that I demand of you, then you will receive my daughter."

"Name what you will," Culhwch calmly replied.

So Ysbaddaden named forty seemingly impossible tasks which Culhwch would have to achieve before he could claim Olwen as his bride.

When the giant at last fell silent, he waited defiantly for Culhwch's reply.

"I will get horses and horsemen, and Arthur, my lord and kinsman will get me all those things you have demanded of me. And I will get your daughter and you will lose your life."

Culhwch spoke resolutely, bowed courteously to the giant, and, with his companions, quietly and resolutely left the court of Ysbaddaden, Chief Giant.

Culhwch is Tested

THE TASKS Ysbaddaden gave to Culhwch were related in different ways to the preparation for the marriage of Culhwch and Olwen and the death of Ysbaddaden. For example, Olwen's wedding veil had to be made from flaxen seed, grown in newly ploughed land, dug, tilled, and planted by the god Amaethon, assisted by the gigantic mythical oxen, known as the Ychen Bannog. Wedding guests were to be offered food from a magic cauldron and drink from an enchanted cup. Music for the wedding was to come from the magic harp of Teirtu, an instrument which could play whatever the listeners wished for and be silent when commanded, and it needed no harpist, it could play itself!

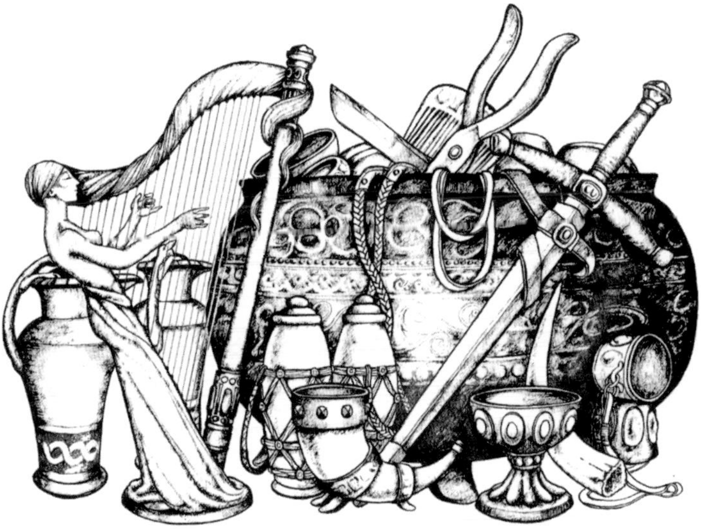

On the night of his impending death, Ysbaddaden would demand food from a hamper which provided whatever anyone could wish for, and it remained full, however much food was taken from it. Before he died, he wished to listen to the birds of Rhiannon sing, birds that could wake the dead and lull the living to sleep.

If Culhwch and Arthur succeeded in accomplishing all these tasks, Ysbaddaden would suffer a gruesome death at the hands of Arthur's men, first he would have his head washed and his beard shaved. The giant's beard and hair was so stiff and strong that only the comb and scissors that were lodged between the ears of the Twrch Trwyth could be used to barber Ysbaddaden before his death. The beard could only be softened and straightened for shaving with the warm blood of the Very Black Witch, the blood itself could only be kept warm in a special bottle.

Many of the most difficult tasks were related to the hunting of the Twrch Trwyth.

The Twrch Trwyth was a gigantic magical boar, at one time a King, son of Lord Tared. He must have offended one of the Celtic gods who had punished him by changing him into a boar. No-one knows any more about this dark past. Destined to live in this shape, the Twrch Trwyth had the sinister reputation for leading the dead into the underworld so he would be a fitting creature to carry the comb razor and scissors that would bring about the death of Ysbaddaden. The Twrch Trwyth and Arthur were old enemies and had already met each other in many previous encounters.

To overcome such a formidable creature, Culhwch and Arthur needed very special assistance from many quarters. Vital to any hunt were the greyhounds. They followed the scent, brought the creature to bay, harassed their prey and helped in the final killing.

Culhwch and Arthur obtained the outstanding hound called Drudwyn, who needed a particular leash belonging to Cors Hundred Claws, and a special collar belonging to Canhastyr Hundred Hands. Drudwyn could only be controlled by Mabon the Hunter, and only one horse was fit for Mabon to ride, this horse was called White Dark Mane, and he was as swift as the waves. Mabon was a god-like hero who had mysteriously disappeared when he was just three nights old. One of Arthur's first tasks was to find Mabon.

Another two young greyhounds born of the bitch Rhymni were shape-changed from human form, and would make spectacular additions to the hunt. These hounds also needed a special leash, plucked from the beard of a giant known as Dillus the Bearded, and it had to be plucked from him while he was alive so that it would be soft and pliable. They were so headstrong that they had to be controlled by Cynedr the Wild, nine times wilder than the wildest beast on the mountain.

Two more hounds, Aned and Aethlem, were indispensable in the hunt, because of their amazing speed; they were described as being as swift as a gust of wind.

In addition to the best hounds and the finest warriors, the huntsmen were equally important. Among these were Garselyd, chief Huntsman of Ireland, Gwyn ap Nudd, the King of the Underworld, and Gwilhenin, King of France.

Of course, the greatest ally Culhwch could have was Arthur himself.

Once captured, the Twrch Trwyth could only be slain by the sword of Wrnach the Giant. Ysbaddaden hoped that Culhwch would surely fail to get all these things before he finally attempted to wrench the comb, razor and scissors from between the ears of the Twrch Trwyth and so win Olwen. Culhwch was determined and confident and together with Arthur and his warriors, they were at last ready for the hunt.

Finding Mabon

CULHWCH, ARTHUR and the warriors left the Giant's fort and gathered together to prepare for the challenging tasks set by Ysbaddaden.

"Where should we begin?" Arthur asked his closest friends Cai and Bedwyr.

"Mabon is one of the greatest hunters, god-like, he was stolen from his mother at birth," Cai replied. "I am sure that we need his help, if we are to succeed in overcoming Ysbaddaden and assisting Culhwch to marry Olwen. I think it is a matter of great importance that we must first of all find Mabon."

Bedwyr agreed with Cai and, at Arthur's request, Cai, Bedwyr, and Gwrhyr set out on this important task.

"Gwrhyr, you speak the languages of the birds and beasts," said Cai, "whom should we ask for advice?"

"The ancient animals of wisdom will help us," said Gwrhyr. "Let us find them."

The three friends came first to the Blackbird of the Wirral, who was older than the people of the Stone Age.

"Do you know anything of the whereabouts of Mabon, stolen from his mother when he was only three days old?" asked Gwrhyr.

"I cannot help you," said the Blackbird, "but I will take you to the Stag of Bracken Hill, older than the first tree, he might know."

The Blackbird guided Cai, Bedwyr and Gwrhyr to the Stag of Bracken Hill.

"Do you know anything of Mabon?" asked Gwrhyr, "he has not been seen since he was snatched from his mother when he was a baby."

"I cannot help you," said the Stag, "but I will take you to the Owl of the Grey Valley, older than the first forests, he may know."

The Stag led them to the Owl of the Grey Valley.

"These are Arthur's messengers," the Stag said to the Owl, "they are seeking Mabon, who has not been seen since he was a baby."

"I am sorry, but I cannot help you," said the Owl, "but I will take you to the Eagle of Alder Heath. He is so old he saw rocks sink below the sea, he may know."

"We have come from Arthur," Gwrhyr said to the Eagle, "to ask if you know anything of Mabon, no-one seems to know his whereabouts and we have great need of him."

"I am sorry I cannot help you," said the Eagle, "I have heard nothing of the man you ask for, but I will take you to the Salmon of Llyn Lliwan, the oldest creature of all time; if he cannot help you I know of no-one else who can."

The Eagle said to the Salmon of Llyn Lliwan, "I have brought Arthur's messengers to you, to ask if you know anything of Mabon, no-one knows where he is and they have great need of him."

"I know a little which may be of some help to you," said the Salmon. "With every flood time, I travel up the great waters, until I come to the bend in the wall of Gloucester, where I have found more wickedness than I have ever found anywhere, the wickedness that has befallen Mabon might well be found in such a place. I will carry you there on my shoulders."

Cai and Gwrhyr sat on the shoulders of the Salmon, and he took them up the waters of the Severn, until they came to Gloucester, where they heard a great moaning in that place, outside the wall of a prison.

"Who is weeping in this hard cruel place?" asked Gwrhyr.

"It is Mabon, sir," the voice cried out, "incarcerated since my birth, and in a more cruel prison than any before me, not even Lludd Silver Hand or Graid, son of Eri, imprisoned by Gwyn ap Nudd, suffered as I have suffered."

"Can you be released by ransom with gold or silver?" asked Gwrhyr.

"I will never be freed except by fighting," replied Mabon.

Gwrhyr and Cai returned to Arthur and reported to him what they had found. Arthur's face was grim and determined as he gathered all his men and rode to the prison at Gloucester. Cai and Bedwyr mounted the shoulders of the great Salmon who bore them once more up the Severn water to rescue Mabon from his cruel incarceration. Arthur's warriors courageously attacked the fort, while Cai broke through the wall of the prison and took Mabon on his back, and continued fighting alongside his friends until they were all victorious and they brought Mabon safely home.

Hunting
the Twrch Trwyth

Ireland - The Hunt Begins

ARTHUR GATHERED all the warriors with their horses, the huntsmen, the hounds, the men and servants and everything they needed for the great hunt. They came from the Islands of Britain, from France, Brittany and from Normandy. When they were all assembled, Arthur and his great army travelled to Ireland in search of the Twrch Trwyth.

After much searching throughout Ireland, Arthur finally found the Twrch with his brood at a place called the Ridge of Coldness. Huntsmen and hounds attacked the creatures vigorously, but the Twrch kept them at bay with his wicked tusks and poisonous bristles, desperate to protect his young brood of seven pigs. Arthur and his warriors fought furiously for nine days and nights and, even then, only managed to kill one small pig.

Of the remaining brood, Grugyn Silver Bristle and Llwydog the Killer were the largest; the other smaller pigs were called Little White Boar, Banwen, Benwig, and Gwys.

Arthur, renowned for his wisdom, sought to avoid unnecessary bloodshed, and asked Gwrhyr, to talk with the Twrch in his language, to find out if the boar did indeed hold the comb, razor and scissors between his ears, and, if so, to ask if he would he be prepared to give them up to Arthur peacefully.

So Gwrhyr went to the Twrch's lair, and asked him to come and talk with Arthur, but the Twrch Trwyth refused and sent Grugyn Silver Bristle to answer for him.

"We will do nothing to help Arthur," said Grugyn. "We have all been condemned to wear this hideous shape; it is enough that we are condemned to such callous injustice, without having to endure your constant threats and insults."

"Arthur will not give up this fight," insisted Gwrhyr. "He has sworn a blood oath to his cousin Culhwch and will never give up until he has redeemed his pledge."

"We will keep all that is rightfully our own, in particular, the comb, the razor and the scissors which the Twrch Trwyth carries between his ears. Those treasures will not be taken from him until they are wrested from him by force or until his life is taken," said Grugyn. "You have already put to death one of our brood, we are now determined to go to Arthur's land to seek revenge. There, we will wreak as much havoc as possible."

There was no more to be said. The Twrch Trwyth plunged into the Irish Sea and made for the Welsh coast, and with him, his litter of six young pigs, all bent on destruction and death.

Arthur lost no time in pursuing the boar in his ship, *Prydwen*.

The Twrch landed at Porth Clais near St. David's Head, in Pembrokeshire, and Arthur's ship came to port in Mynyw near Daugleddyf.

The Twrch charged furiously down towards Daugleddyf, then headed for the farm belonging to a man called Cynwas the Lame, where the boar began destroying the man's cattle. At this point, Arthur caught up with him and forced him to turn and flee, and the beast charged up the hillside in the direction of the Preseli Mountains.

Arthur ordered Eli and Trachmyr, two of his best huntsmen, with a pack of dogs, to follow the Twrch's scent. Eli led the hound, Drudwyn, and men and dogs set up a great noise, beating the ground in front of them, as they stalked the Twrch.

The two dogs of Glythmir, led by Gwarthegyd, strained eagerly at the leash, sniffing in every bush and stream. In the forefront of the hunt, as always, marched Bedwyr, leading Arthur's own dog, Cafall.

Battles in the Preseli Mountains

WAITING AT NEVERN

FINALLY THE huntsmen reached Nevern, where Arthur lined up his champions in battle order, on the two banks of the river.

It was raining heavily, the mountain top veiled by a heavy grey mist and Arthur's men were cold and wet. The warriors listened silently for the signal from the huntsmen that the Twrch's lair had been found. The only sound came from the snorting of the horses as they pawed the ground impatiently. The huntsmen found it difficult to restrain the hounds pulling at the leash, scenting blood. Then the sound of a hunting horn reverberated through the cold, damp mist.

"That is Eli's horn," whispered Bedwyr, "it is time.'

Arthur's champions spurred their horses towards the sound of the hunting horn, followed by the baying hounds.

DISASTER AT CWM CERWYN

The Twrch stood at bay at Cwm Cerwyn. He glared at his enemy with deadly intent, his great tusks and poisonous bristles at the ready. Llwydog the Killer and Grugyn Silver Bristle, two large boar, ranged themselves on either side of the Twrch, the other smaller pigs taking refuge behind his huge body.

The hounds fell on the three great beasts, trying to get at their feet and bite into their backs. The great boar flung them off easily, killing many of the courageous animals with his murderous tusks. Then, men thrust themselves into the fray with spears and swords, some engaging with Llwydog, some with Grugyn and the bravest with the Twrch himself.

So the battle raged that first day, and the Twrch killed four of Arthur's champions, Gwarthegydd, Tarog, Rheiddwn and Isgofan the generous. Then he swerved away trying to escape, but the brave men forced him to make a second stand. The warriors pressed and pushed to get close to the Twrch while the dogs continually goaded the beast. Some of the men used cudgels to rain down blows on his huge flanks, but his hide was tough and well protected by his thick bristles, so that they had little effect. Gwydre, Arthur's son, leapt on the back of the Twrch and with a mighty effort thrust his sword into the rump, but was stuck by the murderous bristles, fell and was trampled to death.

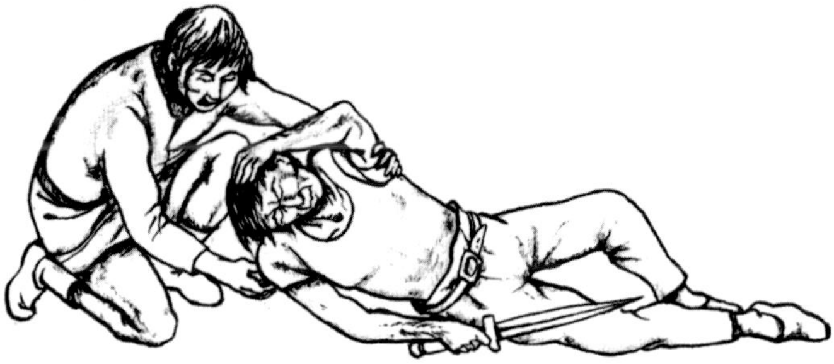

Night fell and darkness forced men and beasts to take cover and take stock of the dead and wounded.

Cacamwri, Arthur's servant, stirred the broth simmering in Arthur's cauldron and tended to the meat roasting on the camp fire. His face was wet with tears. He looked across at the group of men standing soberly at the new cairn of stones. Arthur, Bedwyr, and Hir Peisog, King of Brittany led the mourners as the druid uttered an incantation for dead heroes. Beneath the stones lay the bodies of Gwydre, Arthur's son, and the other heroes who had been poisoned or gored by the murderous Twrch. The mourners moved to their camp fires, Arthur took the bowl of steaming food from Cacamwri's outstretched hands, and smiled sadly at his servant's tearful face.

"Take heart, Cacamwri," he said quietly, "we will continue to run down the Twrch and his brood, with new determination. These heroes will not have died in vain; we can take courage from their fortitude and bravery." His face was grim. "Now we must try to sleep, to recover our strength and face tomorrow with fresh zeal. I will not waver until I have put to death the Twrch and honoured my promise to my kinsman Culhwch."

On the second day, some of the men, enthused by Arthur's stirring words, set off at dawn, ahead of the main army, and surprised the Twrch as he was drinking from a clear stream flowing down the mountainside. In this company were three servants to one of Arthur's

champions, his gate-keeper, Glewlwyd Mighty-Grasp. The baying hounds led them to a large thicket where the creature was hiding, and they hallooed and beat the bushes to force the creature from his lair. Suddenly he charged and the men were ill-equipped to stand up to the might of the Twrch. With his huge tusks, he gored one through the stomach, one in the chest and the third through the spine.

Then he fled on down the rocky hillside seeking cover where he could. Huntsmen urged on the hounds, shouting and calling to them as they rushed hither and thither looking for the scent. All the other wild creatures in that countryside fled from the cry of the hounds and the babble and din of men shouting and horns trumpeting. Men on horseback cast about in crag and thicket, led by the baying of the hounds, beating the bushes and setting up a cacophony of noise of horns and shouts.

Suddenly the Twrch burst out from a thick bushy copse and charged at three of the men hurling them to the ground, where they lay wounded and bleeding, and then he raced off at great speed. Men pursued him, trying to hurl their weapons at his body; spears and arrows rained down on him, but his tough thick hide was protected by his dangerous bristles so that arrows and spears splintered into pieces or glanced off his back and fell harmlessly to the ground.

The Chase Eastwards

PEULINIOG, ABER TYWI AND GLYN YSTUN

SO THE HUNT continued, with many men suffering hideous death and injury and the Twrch rampaged down the hillside past Clunderwen and Llanddewi Velfrey near Whitland and St. Clears. Arthur caught up with him in Peuliniog and there Madog, son of Teithion and Gwyn, son of Tringad died, horribly torn apart by the vicious tusks of the Twrch.

From there, the Twrch raced headlong to Aber Tywi, and the huntsmen and hounds forced him out of his hiding place, a small cave in the rocky hillside.

He confronted his relentless persecutors defiantly, then suddenly charged head-on at his foes. He trampled Cynlas, son of Cynan to death, savagely stuck Gwilenhin, King of France through the abdomen, and then rammed his way through men and dogs to race away once more. Undaunted, the hunters pursued him furiously as far as Glyn Ystun, but then men and hounds lost him.

Arthur summoned Gwyn ap Nudd, King of the Underworld, and asked him if he had any idea had where the Twrch had gone to ground, but the great king said that even he had not been able to track him down.

Arthur's Revenge

THE AMMAN VALLEY

SO THIS GREAT hunt continued and all the huntsmen sought the Twrch through every nook and cranny, hunting the boar and his six pigs as far as Dyffryn Llychwr.

Grugyn Silver Bristle was one of the fiercest of the herd. His poisonous bristles were like silver wire so that the huntsmen could often sight him wherever he fled for cover. Llwydog the Killer, as ferocious as Grugyn, also fought fiercely with Arthur's men, indeed so ferocious was his attack, that he killed all the huntsmen pursuing him, save one.

Arthur and his men now arrived at the place where Grugyn and Llwydog lay in hiding, and they let loose the dogs on the two wild boars. The fighting was so fierce that the baying of the hounds and the noise of the battle brought the great Twrch from his hiding place to come to the aid of his two pigs. In all the time that Arthur's warriors had been pursuing the Twrch, this was the first time that Arthur had actually had sight of the great beast. Arthur's men and dogs quickly picked up the trail as the Twrch turned and headed for the Black Mountain.

Now all of the herd were in disarray and scattered for cover in the heavily wooded valley. They retreated to dark coverts in the thickest part of the forest or hid behind a grassy bank, but they never strayed far from the water. Arthur's men stalked them relentlessly, and suddenly the dogs picked up the scent of one of the pigs. The huntsmen turned to follow the baying hounds who goaded the pig (this one was called Banwen) until it was forced to break cover. The pig rammed its tusks at the dogs and threw one up over its head, but others bit into its back and the men's arrows rained down on the beast until it lay dead.

Another of the pigs, Little Whiteboar, was now forced into the open, he too defended himself ferociously, but to no avail, and soon, he too, was killed.

Maddened by the taste of blood, the lusty dogs trampled through the thick undergrowth and tracked down yet another of the pigs. Their ferocious barking and baying could be heard throughout the countryside as they drove the pig from his hiding place into the open where men and dogs slaughtered him. This one was called Gwys.

Beleaguered by the fury of the hunt, the Twrch was forced to head for Dyffryn Amanw, and there, two more pigs, Banw and Benwig were killed. Of the six pigs that came across the sea with the Twrch, none escaped that battle alive, save Grugyn Silver Bristle and Llwydog the Killer.

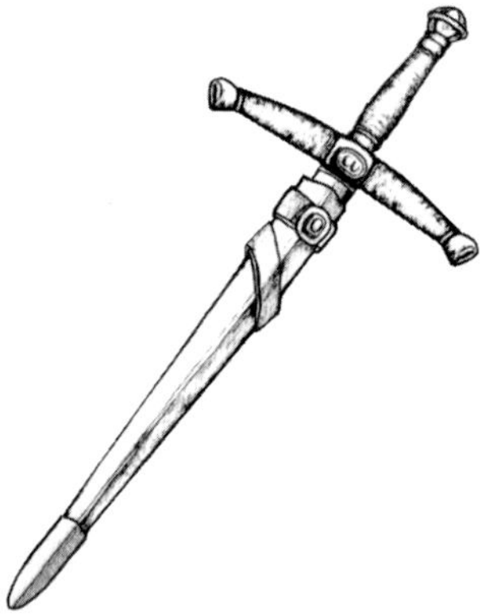

Battles at the Lakes

LLYN LLECH OWAIN

The Twrch charged on to Llyn Llech Owain, where he made a stand. Two of Arthur's warriors, Echel Mighty Thigh and Arwyli, determined to tackle the animal. The beast stood defiantly with the hillside at his back, froth foamed from his mouth as he sharpened his fearful tusks. Echel tried to thrust his sword into the side of the beast's neck but the Twrch turned and bit into the poor man's back and he instantly fell dead.

Undaunted, Arwyli took the Twrch by surprise and thrust at his throat, but he too was no match for the boar; he turned his great body and dispatched the man with his ferocious tusks. Nevertheless, the bowmen broke his stand and forced him into the open. Men and dogs encircled the beleaguered animal, but, by sheer strength, he charged through, killing many men and dogs in his path and fled this way and that, in and out of crags and thickets at the side of the marshland, pursued relentlessly by huntsmen and hounds.

LLYN Y FAN FAWR

Arthur's men galloped across country seeking their prey. The three boars, Grugyn, Llwydog and the Twrch found a temporary respite near Llyn y Fan Fawr, in the Black Mountain. The hounds picked up the scent of the Twrch at the side of a marsh and the huntsmen urged them on with the sound of their horns and much hallooing.

Grugyn was the first to break cover, and turned this way and that to get away from the pack. Arrows rained down on him and he was forced to stand and fight. The hounds fell on his back trying to get their teeth into his hide. He tossed them off, trampling some and killing others with his huge tusks. Eli and Trachmyr were close behind, with the great hound, Drudwyn. With a great effort, Grugyn swerved through men and dogs and fled in the direction of Din Tywi and Ceredigion.

What a noise followed behind as the huntsmen galloped after him, with their dogs racing alongside! Nevertheless, Grugyn was able to keep them at bay until they reached the Ystwyth Valley. At Llanilar, he sought cover in the bushes, but he was forced into the open to face his tormentors.

Then dogs fell on him and arrows rained down on his back. He attacked and killed many brave men; one was Rhyddfyw Rhys, viciously gored through the spine. But the attack continued relentlessly, Grugyn was encircled by hounds and huntsmen, until, finally, he was exhausted, and dispatched by a final sword thrust through the back of his neck. The great beast lay dead, silenced at last.

As Eli surveyed the kill, he said, "What a splendid animal, a worthy prize to bear back to Arthur. Set to, and prepare the beast for the journey home."

A man skilled in woodcraft set to work. The head was cut off first, and fixed on a stake. Then the body divided into two parts, the entrails were extracted and broiled on red hot embers then mixed with bread. These were thrown to the dogs as a reward. The flesh was sliced into broad portions, then the two sides of the carcass fastened together and slung from a sturdy pole. The men then began their journey back to Arthur with the body proudly displayed on the pole, and the head borne on a stake in front of the warrior who had dispatched the final blow.

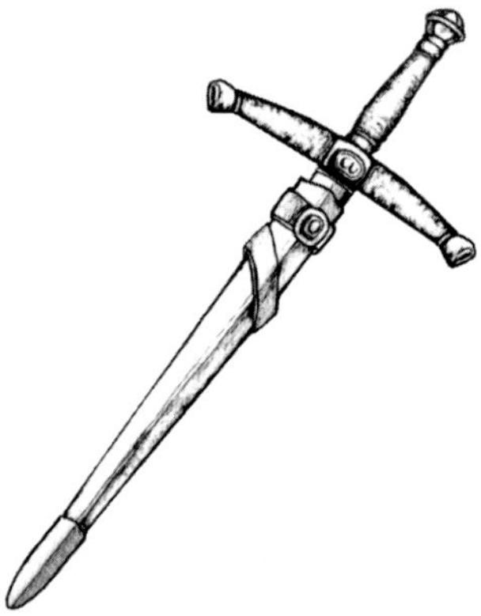

Llwydog Races for Talgarth

YSTRAD YW

WHILE ELI AND TRACHMYR pursued and killed Grugyn Silver Bristle, other huntsmen flushed out Llwydog from his hiding place near Llyn y Fan Fawr, and forced him into the open. Twisting and turning across the countryside, Llwydog fled towards Ystrad Yw, near Talgarth. He was pursued by the men of Brittany, and these brave huntsmen tracked him down until he too was compelled to make a stand.

Llwydog injured many men, before Hir Peisog, the King himself, dismounted, and strode through a stream to where the beast stood at bay. The boar rushed at the man so that man and beast fell in the stream. The King quickly got to his feet, sword in hand, and thrust it into

the animal's thick hide, but Llwydog fell on the King and gored him through the heart. Hir Peisog fell lifeless into the water.

Infuriated by the death of this brave warrior, Emys and Gwrfoddw, attacked Llwydog trying to get at his neck to stick him with their swords. But he turned on them and killed them horribly, with tusks and teeth. Undaunted, other huntsmen continued attacking the creature with arrows, spears and swords until, finally, Llwydog the Killer, exhausted with the fight, was at last put to death.

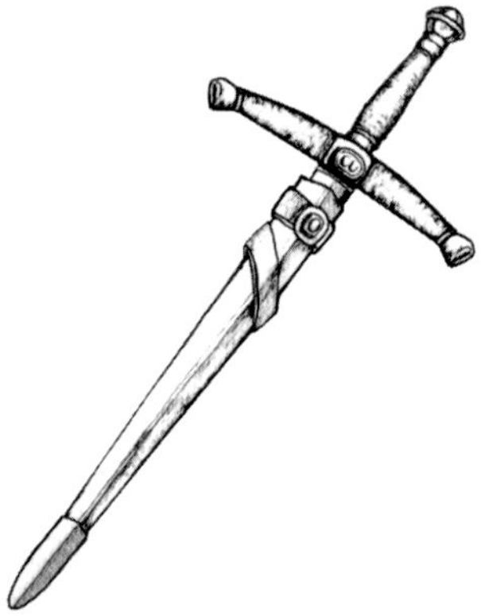

The Twrch is Cornered at the Severn Estuary

THE TWRCH, now alone, continued to drive forward, out of reach of the pursuing horses, men and hounds. The dogs followed his scent as he fled towards the Tawy Valley. He kept out of sight, bolting into thick undergrowth, wherever he could find it, pushing hard to keep out of the reach of the determined advance of Arthur's men. He was making for Ewias in the direction of Llyn Lliwan near the mouth of the Severn.

When Arthur got word of the direction the Twrch was taking, he sent envoys to the leaders of the armies of Cornwall and Devon, asking them to meet him at Llyn Lliwan. These leaders, loyal to King Arthur, swiftly arrived at this point with a vast contingent of warriors and Arthur told them that he believed that the Twrch would try to make his escape towards the West coast.

"I believe that the Twrch intends to escape from Wales and find refuge in your countries," he said. "I want to prevent that happening at all costs. The Twrch has slain so many of my men, I am determined that he will go no further. I will meet him here, at the mouth of the river, where I will keep my promise to Culhwch, and force the comb, razor and scissors from between the creature's ears," he paused, "and then I will kill him. Leaders of Cornwall and Devon, you must do what you will."

The armies of Devon and Cornwall set off on horseback to Ewias and from there to Llyn Lliwan, where they located the hiding place of the Twrch. There they encircled him, using every experienced soldier they possessed, forced him out into the open and drove him by sheer force towards the lake.

So the great boar was driven by the warriors of Cornwall and Devon to the edge of Llyn Lliwan, a tidal lake near the mouth of the river, where Arthur leapt upon the body of the huge beast, while Manawydan, son of Llŷr, and Cacamwri, Arthur's servant, grabbed the animal by its feet and managed to upend him and force him into the tidal waters.

Mabon, son of Modron, spurred his horse into the water and rode right up alongside the Twrch, and, leaning forward, he snatched the razor from his head. Cyledr the Wild rode up on the other side of the struggling creature and wrenched the scissors from between his ears. But before they could get the comb, the Twrch slipped out of Arthur's grasp, and struggling to his feet, he shook off his tormentors and scrambled back onto the land. With the greatest speed he fled across the shore out of reach of his pursuers and fled towards Cornwall.

Cornwall – The Final Battle

UNDETERRED, ARTHUR and his army of warriors pursued him and tracked him down on the Cornish coast. They attacked the beast with all their might, but the creature stood his ground many times, turning on Arthur and his men, and rushing at them with his terrible tusks until the battle ground was dripping with blood. But, at last, Culhwch managed to seize the comb and tear it from between the ears of the Twrch before the creature was chased out of Cornwall and driven headlong into the deep sea. He was never seen again.

Arthur now called a halt to the hunt of the Twrch Trwyth. He had tracked the creature across many parts of the country and had lost many men, his son, his brothers, his uncles and brave champions, including the Kings of France and Brittany. He had finally accomplished the task set by Ysbaddaden to obtain the comb, razor and scissors lodged between the ears of the Twrch. It was time to complete the quest for Olwen.

Arthur Confronts the Very Black Witch

THEN ARTHUR ASKED, "What other tasks are demanded by Ysbaddaden, before he will give his permission for the marriage of Culhwch and Olwen?"

Cacamwri replied: "There is one more. We have to obtain the warm blood of the Very Black Witch, to soften the beard of the giant before he is shaved." He hesitated, "The Very Black Witch lives in a cave in the uplands of hell."

So Arthur set out and came to the place of the witch's cave. And Cacamwri, and his brother Hygwydd, volunteered to go into the cave, on behalf of their king, to seize the witch. They entered the cave, and immediately, the hideous creature attacked them, grabbed Hygwydd by his hair and threw him to the ground, Cacamwri grabbed her hair and pulled the evil hellcat off his brother. Then she turned on Cacamwri and thrashed both brothers with her broomstick; she wrenched their weapons from them, and threw them out on their heads, shrieking and shouting.

Arthur was furious, and wanted to go in himself to settle matters, but Gwyn ap Nudd did not think it was

right for a King as great as Arthur to wrestle with a witch, so they sent in two more servants, the biggest they could find, they were called Hir Amren and Hir Eiddil. But she despatched them with even less ceremony than she had the first two and sent them hurtling out of the cave, bruised and battered.

This made Arthur very angry and he stood at the mouth of the cave and threw his dagger, Carnwennan, through the opening of the cave, at the witch. The blade cut her in two at the waist and the two parts of her body fell to the ground. Then Caw, a warrior from North Britain took the warm blood of the Very Black Witch put it into a bottle and kept it until the time came to use it.

Death and Celebration

Culhwch, Caw, Goreu, son of Custennin, and other men who hated Ysbaddaden, set off to the giant's castle, taking the scissors, the comb, the razor and the warm blood of the Very Black Witch with them. Caw shaved the giant's beard, skin and flesh clean off to the bone from ear to ear.

"Are you prepared to meet your death?" said Culhwch.

"I have no choice," said Ysbaddaden, sullenly.

"Is your daughter mine now?" continued Culhwch

"Yes, she is yours," said the giant, grudgingly, "but I do not give her willingly, I would never have given my permission, and your success is entirely due to your cousin, Arthur. If I had my way, you would never have had her, for when I part with her, I lose my life."

Goreu, son of Custennin, could wait no longer; he was impatient to avenge the deaths of his brothers. He seized Ysbaddaden by the hair of his head and dragged him to the keep of the castle. There he cut off the giant's head and placed it on a stake on the citadel.

Then Arthur took possession of Ysbaddaden's castle and all his treasures and the quest for Olwen was complete.

That night the beautiful maiden became Culhwch's bride, and she continued to be his wife as long as she lived.

Thus did Culhwch obtain Olwen, the daughter of Ysbaddaden, Chief Giant.

Bibliography

Barber, Richard, *The Arthurian Legends,* Boydell Press, 1979 (reissued in paperback, 1987).

Barber, Chris and Williams, John Godfrey, *Ancient Stones of Wales,* Blorenge Books, 1989.

Barber, Chris, *Mysterious Wales,* David & Charles, Newton Abbot, 1986.

Barber, Chris, *More Mysterious Wales,* David & Charles, Newton Abbot, 1986.

Bollard, John K. tr. (Griffiths Anthony, photography), *The Mabinogi Legend and Landscape of Wales,* Gomer Press, 2006.

Borrow, George, *Wild Wales,* Collins, 1862 (latest reprint 1977).

Bromwich, Rachel, *The Triads of the Islands of Britain,* University of Wales Press, 2006.

Bullfinch, Thomas, *Age of Chivalry,* Macmillan, 1997.

Children, George and Nash, George, *Prehistoric Sites of Monmouthshire,* Logaston Press, 1996.

Crossley-Holland, Kevin, *The Norse Myths,* Penguin Books, 1982.

Davies, Sioned, *The Four Branches of the Mabinogi,* Gomer Press, 1993.

Davies, Sioned, *The Mabinogion,* Oxford University Press, 2007.

Davies, Elwyn, *A Gazeteer of Welsh Place Names,* University of Wales Press, 1967.

Dixon-Kennedy, Mike, *Heroes of the Round Table,* Blandford, 1997.

Dyer, James, *Hillforts of England and Wales,* Shire Publications Ltd., 1981.

Foss, Michael, *The World of Camelot,* Michael O'Mara Books Limited, 1995.

Gantz, Jeffrey, *The Mabinogion,* Penguin Books, 1976.

Gardner, Don, *Discovering Mid-Wales,* John Jones Cardiff Ltd., 1978.

Green, Miranda Jane, *Celtic Myths,* The British Museum Press, 2000.

Green, Miranda and Howell, Ray, *Celtic Wales,* University of Wales Press, 2000.

Guest, Lady Charlotte, tr. *The Mabinogion,* Dover Thrift, 1997.

Gwyndaf, Robin, *Welsh Folk Tales,* Cardiff: National Museum of Wales, 1989.

Rieu, E. V., tr. *Homer The Odyssey,* Penguin Books Ltd., 1977.

Jones, Gwyn, *Welsh Legends and Folk Tales*, Puffin Books, 1988.
Jones, Gwyn, *Kings, Beasts and Heroes*, Oxford University Press, 1972.
Jones, Gwyn and Jones, Thomas, tr. *The Mabinogion* (revised edition), J. M. Dent and Sons Ltd., 1989.
Jones, T. Gwyn, *Welsh Folk-lore and Folk Custom*, Methuen, 1930.
Lady Gregory, *Irish Mythology*, Bounty Books, 2000.
Main, Lawrence and Coates, Neil, *Mid-Wales and the Marches Walks*, Jarrold Publishing, 2004.
Ngai, Tai Korero, *Maori Legends*, Reed Publishing Ltd., 2000.
Owen, Hywel Wyn, *The Place Names of Wales*, University of Wales Press, 1998.
Rhys, Anthony, *Celtic Legends of Pembrokeshire*, Llanerch Publishers, Felinfach, 1999.
Rhys, Sir John Celtic Folklore: Welsh and Manx, Vols 1-2, Clarendon Press, Oxford, 1901 (Wildwood House, 1980).
Rieu E. V., tr. revised Peter Jones, *Homer The Iliad*, Penguin Classics, 2003.
Ritchie, W. F and J. N. G., *Celtic Warriors*, Shire Publications, 1985.
Roberts, Tony, *Castles and Ancient Monuments of West Wales*, Abercastle Publications, 1989.
Robins, Christopher, *A Walk through Wales and its History*, Village Publishing, 1990.
Rutherford, Ward, *Celtic Mythology*, Aquarian Press, 1987.
Stone, Moira K., *Mid Wales Companion*, Anthony Nelson, 1989.
Thomas, Gwyn and Crossley-Holland, Kevin, Jones, Margaret (Illustrations), *Quest for Olwen*, Lutterworth Press, 1988.
Thorpe, Lewis, tr. *Geoffrey of Monmouth The History of the Kings of Britain*, Penguin Books, 1979.
Thorpe, Lewis, tr. *Gerald of Wales: The Journey through Wales/The Description of Wales*, Penguin Classics, 1978 (Reprint 1988).
Thorpe, Lewis, tr. *Hywel Dda The Law*, Gomer Press, 1986.
Tolkien, J. R. R. and Gordon, E. V., *Sir Gawain and The Green Knight*, Oxford Clarendon Press, 1925.
Ward, Frank, *The Lakes of Wales*, Herbert Jenkins Limited, 1931.
White, Richard, *Gerald's Wales*, CADW, 1988.
Williams, Herbert, *Stories of King Arthur*, John Jones, 1990.

Maps

Rees, William, *An Historical Atlas of Wales from Early to Modern Times*, William Lewis (Printers), 1951.

Ordnance Survey Maps

Road map 6 Wales/Cymru & West Midlands, 1:250 000 scale.
Explorer Map OL35 North Pembrokeshire, 1:25 000 scale.
Explorer Map OL36 South Pembrokeshire, 1:25 000 scale.
Explorer Map OL185 Newcastle Emlyn, 1:25 000 scale.
Explorer Map OL 177 Carmarthen and Kidwelly, 1:25 000 scale.
Explorer Map OL 178 Llanelli and Ammanford, 1:25 000 scale.
Explorer Map OL12 Brecon Beacons National Park, Western area, 1:25 000.
Explorer Map OL13 Brecon Beacons National Park, Eastern area, 1:25 000 scale.
Explorer Map OL14 Wye Valley and Forest of Dean, 1:25 000 scale.

Other books by APECS Press

TALES OF GOLD

Margaret Isaac

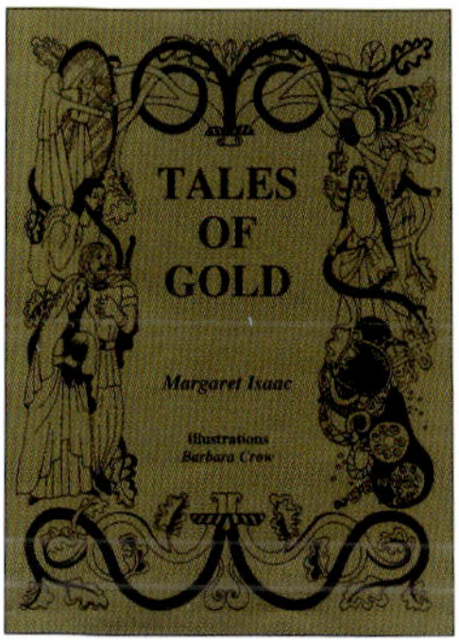

A collection of five short stories of caves, gold and treasure. They include sleeping knights, a childhood dream, a wizard, a dragon, and a magical golden harp.

A Welsh Books Council Reader comments: "This collection is a treasure which deserves to be accessible to twenty-first century children and beyond."

"The writing reminds me of C. S. Lewis The Chronicles of Narnia . . ."

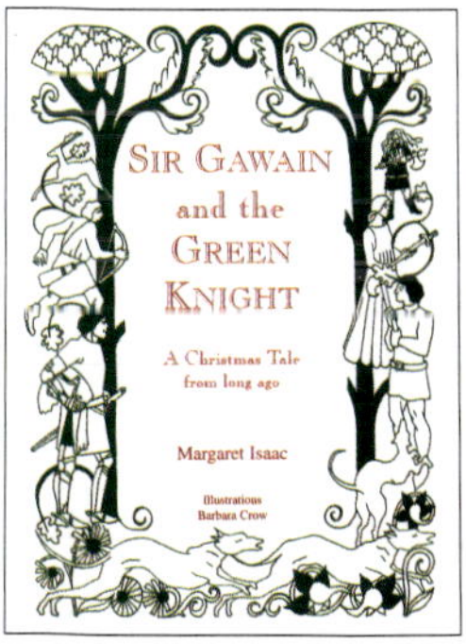

SIR GAWAIN AND THE GREEN KNIGHT

Margaret Isaac

Sir Gawain, as Arthur's champion, faces dishonour and death at the hands of the Green Knight.

An entertaining Christmas story with unexpected twists and turns told with humour and compassion.

RHIANNON'S WAY

Margaret Isaac

Caradog, a Celtic Chieftain, has been captured by the Romans.
Rhiannon, his daughter, tries to rescue him with the help of her friend Brychan, her pony Llwyd and the magic of the Mabinogi.
An exciting tale set against the backdrop of the brutal Roman regime in Wales.

LAKE STORIES OF WALES

Shadows in the Waters

Margaret Isaac

Five enchanting stories of lakes in south Wales about threatening water spirits, a cruel princess, Arthur's greatest knight, the lady of healing and magic and the true prince of Wales. (also published in Welsh).

THE TALE OF TWM SIÔN CATI

Margaret Isaac

Twm Sion Cati uses all his skills of disguise and mimicry in his courageous escapades against the evil squire, Jasper Tyler, and the cruel Elias Richards.
A tale of wild Wales under the oppressive regime of Henry V111.

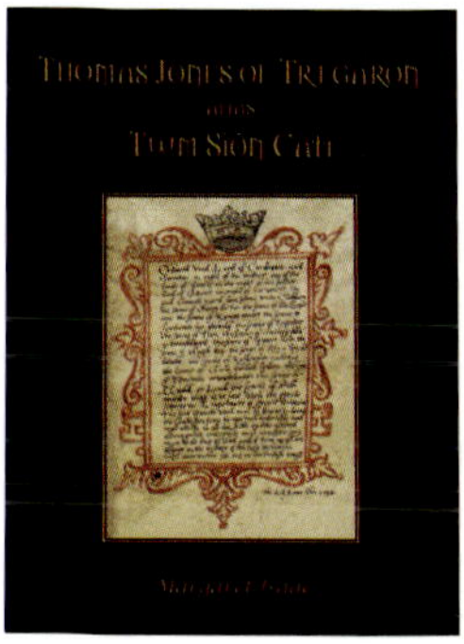

THOMAS JONES OF TREGARON ALIAS TWM SION CATI

Margaret Isaac

Thomas Jones of Tregaron was pardoned by Elizabeth 1. He became a poet, heraldic bard and respected squire of Tregaron.
The book contains copies of manuscripts of his beautifully crafted pedigrees.

IT CAME TO PASS – *An Autobiography*

Margaret Jones

It was my good fortune, in the twenty years from 1980, to illustrate for publication, a number of the great traditional tales of the world, especially my adoptive country of Wales. Now I am urged to write an account of how that came to pass. I have had a generous slice of life's cake and I have eaten every crumb with relish. It would be nice if we could have our cake and eat it, but I wouldn't bank on it, indeed I think such a marvel is as much of a fairy tale as any I have pictured for children's books. So I will do as I have been urged to do and make my meagre record here. Memories are like the tide going out on a beach leaving behind little pools and puddles in which we may fish for souvenirs of our holidays. This narrative will be just a bucketful of assorted flotsam.

THOMAS THOMAS OF PONTYPOOL

Arthur Edwards

Thomas Thomas was an ardent dissenter, a zealous social reformer and a passionate supporter of education for the masses. He combined the role of an educator with that of an evangelist. An inspiring teacher, he was also an able organiser who supported the causes affecting the community and many of the battles he fought were against the role and authority of the State church.

BIRTH OF A SCHOOL

J. Alan Shewring

This is the story of how St. Joseph's R.C. School, Newport, started. It charts the successful struggle by a small group of parents to persuade the authorities, both State and Church, that a Catholic comprehensive school was needed in Newport. Also how they, the parents, and the School Governors, succeeded in getting the school built.

DOLAUCOTHI GOLD – *A VISION REALISED*

Alun Isaac

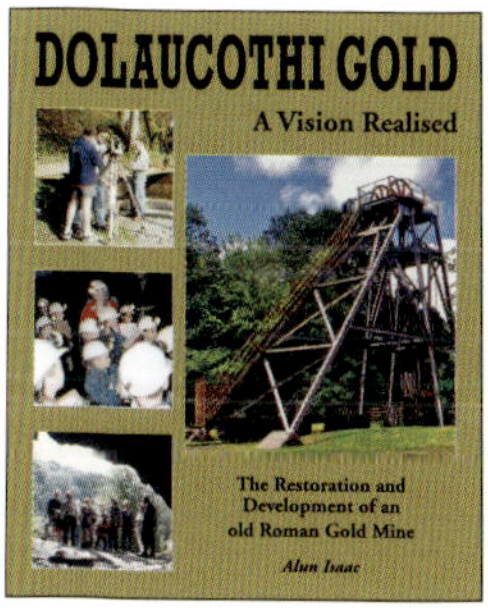

This book provides the definitive record of the restoration and development of the Dolaucothi Gold Mine at Pumsaint, south Wales. This was achieved by a partnership between the National Trust, the University of Wales, Cardiff, Gwent College of Higher Education and the community of Pumsaint and District.

The Twrch

Aberystwyth
Llanbedr Pont Steffan
Lampeter
Aberteifi
Cardigan
4 Nanhyfer
Nevern
Preseli
Cwm Cerwyn
5
2 Penmaendewi
St David's Head
1 Porthglais
Porth Clais
Hwlffordd
Haverfordwest
3
Aberdaugleddau
Milford Haven
Dinbych-y-pysgod
Tenby
Sanclêr
St Clears
6
Caerfyrddin
Carmarthen
7
Abertywi
11
Llanelli

Trwyth Trail

www.aattt.org.uk